C000246084

1 3 5 7 9 10 8 6 4 2

Vintage
20 Vauxhall Bridge Road,
London SW1V 2SA

Vintage Classics is part of the Penguin Random House
group of companies whose addresses can be found at
global.penguinrandomhouse.com

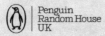
Penguin
Random House
UK

Extract from *In Search of Lost Time, Volume V* translation
copyright © Chatto & Windus and Random House Inc. 1981
Copyright in revisions to translation © D. J. Enright 1992

First published in Great Britain in 1992 by Chatto & Windus
First published by Vintage in 1996
This short edition published by Vintage in 2017

penguin.co.uk/vintage

A CIP catalogue record for this book is available from the British Library

ISBN 9781784872694

Typeset in 9.5/14.5 pt FreightText Pro
by Jouve (UK), Milton Keynes
Printed and bound by Clays Ltd, St Ives plc

Penguin Random House is committed to a sustainable future for
our business, our readers and our planet. This book is made from
Forest Stewardship Council® certified paper.

MIX
Paper from
responsible sources
FSC
www.fsc.org
FSC® C018179

# Jealousy

## MARCEL PROUST

*Translated from the French by C. K. Scott Moncrieff
and Terence Kilmartin
Revised by D. J. Enright*

**VINTAGE** MINIS

No doubt, in the first days at Balbec, Albertine seemed to exist on a parallel plane to that on which I was living, but one that had converged on it (after my visit to Elstir) and had finally joined it, as my relations with her, at Balbec, in Paris, then at Balbec again, grew more intimate. Moreover, what a difference there was between the two pictures of Balbec, on my first visit and on my second, pictures composed of the same villas from which the same girls emerged by the same sea! In Albertine's friends at the time of my second visit, whom I knew so well, whose good and bad qualities were so clearly engraved on their features, how could I recapture those fresh, mysterious strangers who once could not thrust open the doors of their chalets with a screech over the sand or brush past the quivering tamarisks without making my heart beat? Their huge eyes had sunk into their faces since then, doubtless because they had ceased to be children, but also because those ravishing strangers, those actresses of that first romantic year, about whom I had gone ceaselessly in quest of information, no longer held any mystery for me. They had become for me, obedient to my whims, a mere grove of budding girls, from among whom I was not a little proud of having plucked, and hidden away from the rest of the world, the fairest rose.

Between the two Balbec settings, so different one from the other, there was the interval of several years in Paris, the long expanse of which was dotted with all the visits that Albertine had paid me. I saw her in the different years of my life occupying, in relation to myself, different positions which made me feel the beauty of the intervening spaces, that long lapse of time during which I had remained without seeing her and in the diaphanous depths of which the roseate figure that I saw before me was carved with mysterious shadows and in bold relief. This was due also to the superimposition not merely of the successive images which Albertine had been for me, but also of the great qualities of intelligence and heart, and of the defects of character, all alike unsuspected by me, which Albertine, in a germination, a multiplication of herself, a fleshy efflorescence in sombre colours, had added to a nature that formerly could scarcely have been said to exist, but was now difficult to plumb. For other people, even those of whom we have dreamed so much that they have come to seem no more than pictures, figures by Benozzo Gozzoli against a greenish background, of whom we were inclined to believe that they varied only according to the point of vantage from which we looked at them, their distance from us, the effect of light and shade, such people, while they change in relation to ourselves, change also in themselves, and there had been an enrichment, a solidification and an increase of volume in the figure once simply outlined against the sea.

Moreover, it was not only the sea at the close of day that existed for me in Albertine, but at times the drowsy murmur of the sea upon the shore on moonlit nights. For sometimes, when I got up to fetch a book from my father's study, my mistress, having asked my permission to lie down while I was out of the room, was so tired after her long outing in the morning and afternoon in the open air that, even if I had been away for a moment only, when I returned I found her asleep and did not wake her. Stretched out at full length on my bed, in an attitude so natural that no art could have devised it, she reminded me of a long blossoming stem that had been laid there; and so in a sense she was: the faculty of dreaming, which I possessed only in her absence, I recovered at such moments in her presence, as though by falling asleep she had become a plant. In this way, her sleep realised to a certain extent the possibility of love: alone, I could think of her, but I missed her, I did not possess her; when she was present, I spoke to her, but was too absent from myself to be able to think of her; when she was asleep, I no longer had to talk, I knew that I was no longer observed by her, I no longer needed to live on the surface of myself.

By shutting her eyes, by losing consciousness, Albertine had stripped off, one after another, the different human personalities with which she had deceived me ever since the day when I had first made her acquaintance. She was animated now only by the unconscious life of plants, of trees, a life more different from my own, more alien, and yet one that belonged more to me. Her personality was not constantly escaping, as when we talked, by the outlets of her unacknowledged thoughts and of her eyes. She had called back into herself everything of her that lay outside, had withdrawn, enclosed, reabsorbed herself into her body. In keeping her in front of my eyes, in my hands, I had an impression of possessing her entirely which I never had when she was awake. Her life was submitted to me, exhaled towards me its gentle breath.

I listened to this murmuring, mysterious emanation, soft as a sea breeze, magical as a gleam of moonlight, that was her sleep. So long as it lasted, I was free to dream about her and yet at the same time to look at her, and, when that sleep grew deeper, to touch, to kiss her. What I felt then was a love as pure, as immaterial, as mysterious, as if I had been in the presence of those inanimate creatures which are the beauties of nature. And indeed, as soon as her sleep became at all deep, she ceased to be merely the plant that she had been; her sleep, on the margin of which I remained musing, with a fresh delight of which I never tired, which I could have gone on enjoying indefinitely, was to me a whole landscape. Her sleep brought within my

**In keeping her in front of my eyes, my hands, I had an impression of possessing her entirely which I never had when she was awake**

reach something as serene, as sensually delicious as those nights of full moon on the bay of Balbec, calm as a lake over which the branches barely stir, where, stretched out upon the sand, one could listen for hours on end to the surf breaking and receding.

On entering the room, I would remain standing in the doorway, not venturing to make a sound, and hearing none but that of her breath rising to expire upon her lips at regular intervals, like the reflux of the sea, but drowsier and softer. And at the moment when my ear absorbed that divine sound, I felt that there was condensed in it the whole person, the whole life of the charming captive outstretched there before my eyes. Carriages went rattling past in the street, but her brow remained as smooth and untroubled, her breath as light, reduced to the simple expulsion of the necessary quantity of air. Then, seeing that her sleep would not be disturbed, I would advance cautiously, sit down on the chair that stood by the bedside, then on the bed itself.

I spent many a charming evening talking and playing with Albertine, but none so sweet as when I was watching her sleep. Granted that she had, as she chatted with me, or played cards, a naturalness that no actress could have imitated; it was a more profound naturalness, as it were at one remove, that was offered me by her sleep. Her hair, falling along her pink cheek, was spread out beside her on the bed, and here and there an isolated straight tress gave the same effect of perspective as those moonlit trees, lank and pale, which one sees standing erect and stiff in the back-grounds of Elstir's Raphaelesque pictures. If Albertine's lips were closed, her eyelids, on the other hand, seen from where I was placed, seemed so loosely joined that I might almost have questioned whether she really was asleep. At the same time those lowered lids gave her face that perfect continuity which is unbroken by the eyes. There are people whose faces assume an unaccustomed beauty and majesty the moment they cease to look out of their eyes.

I would run my eyes over her, stretched out below me. From time to time a slight, unaccountable tremor ran through her, as the leaves of a tree are shaken for a few moments by a sudden breath of wind. She would touch her hair and then, not having arranged it to her liking, would raise her hand to it again with motions so consecutive, so deliberate, that I was convinced that she was about to wake. Not at all; she grew calm again in the sleep from which she had not emerged. Thereafter she lay motionless. She had laid her hand on her breast, the limpness of the arm so artlessly childlike that I was obliged, as I gazed at her, to suppress the smile that is provoked in us by the solemnity, the innocence and the grace of little children.

I, who was acquainted with many Albertines in one per-son, seemed now to see many more again reposing by my side. Her eyebrows, arched as I had never noticed them, encircled the globes of her eyelids like a halcyon's downy nest. Races, atavisms, vices reposed upon her face. When-ever she moved her head, she created a different woman, often one whose existence I had never suspected. I seemed to possess not one but countless girls. Her breathing, as it became gradually deeper, made her breast rise and fall in a regular rhythm, and above it her folded hands and her pearls, displaced in a different way by the same movement, like boats and mooring chains set swaying by the movement of the tide. Then, feeling that the tide of her sleep was full, that I should not run aground on reefs of consciousness covered now by the high water of profound slumber, I would climb deliberately and noiselessly on to the bed, lie down by her side, clasp her waist in one arm, and place my lips upon her cheek and my free hand on her heart and then on every part of her body in turn, so that it too was raised, like the pearls, by her breathing; I myself was gently rocked by its regular motion: I had embarked upon the tide of Albertine's sleep.

Sometimes it afforded me a pleasure that was less pure. For this I had no need to make any movement, but allowed my leg to dangle against hers, like an oar which one trails in the water, imparting to it now and again a gentle oscillation like the intermittent wing-beat of a bird asleep in the air. I chose, in gazing at her, the aspect of her face which one never saw and which was so beautiful. It is I suppose comprehensible that the letters which we receive from a person should be more or less similar to one another and combine to trace an image of the writer sufficiently different from the person we know to constitute a second personality. But how much stranger is it that a woman should be conjoined, like Radica with Doodica, with another woman whose different beauty makes us infer another character, and that in order to see them we must look at one of them in profile and the other in full face. The sound of her breathing, which had grown louder, might have given the illusion of the panting of sexual pleasure, and when mine was at its climax, I could kiss her without having interrupted her sleep. I felt at such moments that I had possessed her more completely, like an unconscious and unresisting object of dumb nature. I was not troubled by the words that she murmured from time to time in her sleep; their meaning was closed to me, and besides, whoever the unknown person to whom they referred, it was upon my hand, upon my cheek that her hand, stirred by an occasional faint tremor, tightened for an instant. I savoured her sleep with a disinterested, soothing love, just as I would remain for hours listening to the unfurling of the waves.

Perhaps people must be capable of making us suffer intensely before they can procure for us, in the hours of remission, the same soothing calm as nature does. I did not have to answer her as when we were engaged in conversation, and even if I could have remained silent, as for that matter I did when it was she who was talking, still while listening to her I did not penetrate so far into the depths of her being. As I continued to hear, to capture from moment to moment, the murmur, soothing as a barely perceptible breeze, of her pure breath, it was a whole physiological existence that was spread out before me, at my disposal; just as I used to remain for hours lying on the beach, in the moonlight, so long could I have remained there gazing at her, listening to her. Sometimes it was as though the sea was beginning to swell, as though the storm was making itself felt even inside the bay, and I would press myself against her and listen to the gathering roar of her breath.

Sometimes, when she was too warm, she would take off her kimono while she was already almost asleep and fling it over an armchair. As she slept I would tell myself that all her letters were in the inner pocket of this kimono, into which she always thrust them. A signature, an assignation, would have sufficed to prove a lie or to dispel a suspicion. When I could see that Albertine was sound asleep, leaving the foot of the bed where I had been standing motionless in contemplation of her, I would take a step forward, seized by a burning curiosity, feeling that the secret of this other life lay offering itself to me, flaccid and defenceless, in that armchair. Perhaps I took this step forward also because to stand perfectly still and watch her sleeping became tiring after a while. And so, on tiptoe, constantly turning round to make sure that Albertine was not waking, I would advance towards the armchair. There I would stop short, and stand for a long time gazing at the kimono, as I had stood for a long time gazing at Albertine. But (and here perhaps I was wrong) never once did I touch the kimono, put my hand in the pocket, examine the letters. In the end, realising that I would never make up my mind, I would creep back to the bedside and begin again to watch the sleeping Albertine, who would tell me nothing, whereas I could see lying across an arm of the chair that kimono which would perhaps have told me much.

And just as people pay a hundred francs a day for a room at the Grand Hotel at Balbec in order to breathe the sea air, I felt it to be quite natural that I should spend more than that on her, since I had her breath upon my cheek, between my lips which I laid half-open upon hers, through which her life flowed against my tongue.

But this pleasure of seeing her sleep, which was as sweet to me as that of feeling her live, was cut short by another pleasure, that of seeing her wake. It was, carried to a more profound and more mysterious degree, the same pleasure as I felt in having her under my roof. It was gratifying to me, of course, that when she alighted from the car in the afternoon, it should be to my house that she was returning. It was even more so to me that when, from the underworld of sleep, she climbed the last steps of the staircase of dreams, it was in my room that she was reborn to consciousness and life, that she wondered for an instant: 'Where am I?' and, seeing the objects by which she was surrounded, and the lamp whose light scarcely made her blink her eyes, was able to assure herself that she was at home on realising that she was waking in *my* home. In that first delicious moment of uncertainty, it seemed to me that once again I was taking possession of her more completely, since, instead of her returning to her own room after an outing, it was my room that, as soon as Albertine should have recognised it, was about to enclose, to contain her, without there being any sign of misgiving in her eyes, which remained as calm as if she had never slept at all. The uncertainty of awakening, revealed by her silence, was not at all revealed in her eyes.

Then she would find her tongue and say: 'My—' or 'My darling —' followed by my first name, which, if we give the narrator the same name as the author of this book, would be 'My Marcel,' or 'My darling Marcel.' After this I would never allow a member of my family, by calling me 'darling,' to rob of their precious uniqueness the delicious words that Albertine uttered to me. As she uttered them, she pursed her lips in a little pout which she spontaneously transformed into a kiss. As quickly as she had earlier fallen asleep, she had awoken.

No MORE THAN my own progression in time, no more than the fact of looking at a girl sitting near me beneath a lamp that shed upon her a very different light from that of the sun when I used to see her striding along the seashore, was this material enrichment, this autonomous progress of Albertine, the determining cause of the difference between my present view of her and my original impression of her at Balbec. A longer term of years might have separated the two images without effecting so complete a change; it had come about, this sudden and fundamental change, when I had learned that Albertine had been virtually brought up by Mlle Vinteuil's friend. If at one time I had been overcome with excitement when I thought I detected mystery in Albertine's eyes, now I was happy only at times when from those eyes, from those cheeks even, as revealing as the eyes, at one moment so gentle but quickly turning sullen, I succeeded in expelling every trace of mystery. The image which I sought, upon which I relied, for which I would have been prepared to die, was no longer that of Albertine leading an unknown life, it was that of an Albertine as known to me as it was possible for her to be (and it was for this reason that my love could not be lasting unless it remained unhappy, for by definition it did not satisfy the need for mystery), an Albertine who did not reflect a distant world, but desired nothing else—there were moments when this did indeed appear to be the case—than to be with me, to be exactly like me, an Albertine who was the image precisely of what was mine and not of the unknown.

When it is thus from an hour of anguish in relation to another person that love is born, when it is from uncertainty whether we shall keep or lose that person, such a love bears the mark of the revolution that has created it, it recalls very little of what we had previously seen when we thought of the person in question. And although my first impressions of Albertine, silhouetted against the sea, might to some small extent persist in my love for her, in reality, these earlier impressions occupy but a tiny place in a love of this sort, in its strength, in its agony, in its need of comfort and its resort to a calm and soothing memory with which we would prefer to abide and to learn nothing more of the beloved, even if there were something horrible to be known. Even if the previous impressions are retained, such a love is made of very different stuff!

Sometimes I would put out the light before she came in. It was in the darkness, barely guided by the glow of a smouldering log, that she would lie down by my side. My hands and my cheeks alone identified her without my eyes seeing her, my eyes that were often afraid of finding her changed; so that, by virtue of these blind caresses, she may perhaps have felt bathed in a warmer tenderness than usual.

On other evenings, I undressed and went to bed, and, with Albertine perched on the side of the bed, we would resume our game or our conversation interrupted by kisses; and in the physical desire that alone makes us take an interest in the existence and character of another person, we remain so true to our own nature (even if, on the other hand, we abandon successively the different persons whom we have loved in turn) that on one occasion, catching sight of myself in the mirror at the moment when I was kissing Albertine and calling her 'my little girl,' the sorrowful, passionate expression on my own face, similar to the expression it would have worn long ago with Gilberte whom I no longer remembered, and would perhaps assume one day with another if I were ever to forget

Albertine, made me think that, over and above any personal considerations (instinct requiring that we consider the person of the moment as the only real one), I was performing the duties of an ardent and painful devotion dedicated as an oblation to the youth and beauty of Woman. And yet with this desire by which I was honouring youth with a votive offering, with my memories too of Balbec, there was blended, in my need to keep Albertine thus every evening by my side, something that had hitherto been foreign to my amorous existence at least, if it was not entirely new in my life. It was a soothing power the like of which I had not experienced since the evenings at Combray long ago when my mother, stooping over my bed, brought me repose in a kiss. To be sure, I should have been greatly astonished at that time had anyone told me that I was not extremely kind and especially that I would ever seek to deprive someone else of a pleasure. I must have known myself very imperfectly then, for my pleasure in having Albertine to live with me was much less a positive pleasure than the pleasure of having withdrawn from the world, where everyone was free to enjoy her in turn, the blossoming girl who, if she did not bring me any great joy, was at least withholding joy from others. Ambition and fame would have left me unmoved. Even more was I incapable of feeling hatred. And yet to love carnally was none the less, for me, to enjoy a triumph over countless rivals. I can never repeat it often enough: it was more than anything else an appeasement.

For all that I might, before Albertine returned, have doubted her, have imagined her in the room at Montjouvain, once she was in her dressing-gown and seated facing my chair or (if, as was more frequent, I had remained in bed) at the foot of my bed, I would deposit my doubts in her, hand them over for her to relieve me of them, with the abnegation of a worshipper uttering a prayer. All through the evening she might have been there, curled up in a mischievous ball on my bed, playing with me like a cat; her little pink nose, the tip of which she made even tinier with a coquettish glance which gave it a daintiness characteristic of certain women who are inclined to be plump, might have given her an inflamed and provocative air, she might have allowed a tress of her long, dark hair to fall over her pale-pink waxen cheek and, half shutting her eyes, unfolding her arms, have seemed to be saying to me: 'Do what you like with me'—but when the time came for her to leave me, and she drew close to me to say good-night, it was a softness that had become almost familial that I kissed on either side of her sturdy neck which then never seemed to me brown or freckled enough, as though these solid qualities were associated with a certain frank good nature in Albertine.

'Are you coming with us tomorrow, old crosspatch?' she would ask before leaving me.

'Where are you going?'

'That will depend on the weather and on you. But have you written anything today, my little darling? No? Then it was hardly worth your while not coming with us. Tell me, by the way, when I came in this evening, you knew my step, you guessed at once who it was?'

'Of course. Could I possibly be mistaken? Couldn't I tell my little goose's footstep among a thousand? She must let me take her shoes off before she goes to bed, it will give me such pleasure. You're so nice and pink in all that white lace.'

Such was my answer, amid the sensual expressions, others will be recognised that were peculiar to my grandmother and my mother. For, little by little, I was beginning to resemble all my relations: my father who—in a very different fashion from myself, no doubt, for if things repeat themselves, it is with great variations—took so keen an interest in the weather; and not my father only, but, more and more, my aunt Léonie. Otherwise Albertine could not but have been a reason for my going out, so as not to leave her on her own, beyond my control. Although every day I found an excuse in some particular indisposition, what made me so often remain in bed was a person—not Albertine, not a person I loved but a person with more power over me than any beloved—who had transmigrated into me, a person despotic to the point of silencing at times my jealous suspicions or at least of preventing me from going to verify whether they had any foundation, and that person was my aunt Léonie—my aunt Léonie, who was entirely steeped in piety and with whom I could have sworn that I had not a single point in common, I who was so passionately fond of pleasure, apparently worlds apart from that maniac who had never known any pleasure in her life and lay telling her beads all day long, I who suffered from my inability to actualise a literary career whereas she had been the one person in the family who could never understand that reading was anything other than a means of whiling away the time, of 'amusing oneself,' which made it, even at Eastertide, permissible on Sundays, when every serious occupation is forbidden in order that the whole day may be hallowed by prayer. And as if it were not enough that I should bear an exaggerated resemblance to my father, to the extent of not being satisfied like him with consulting the barometer, but becoming an animated barometer myself, as if it were not enough that I should allow myself to be ordered by my aunt Léonie to stay at home and watch the weather, from my bedroom window or even from my bed, here I was talking now to Albertine, at one moment as the child that I had been at Combray used to talk to my mother, at another as my grandmother used to talk to me. When we have passed a certain age, the soul of the child that we were and the souls of the dead from whom we sprang come and shower upon us their riches and their spells, asking to be allowed to contribute to the new emotions which we feel and in which, erasing their former image, we recast them in an original creation. Thus my whole past from my earliest years, and, beyond these, the past of my parents and relations, blended with my impure love for Albertine the tender charm of an affection at once filial and maternal. We have to give hospitality, at a certain stage in our lives, to all our relatives who have journeyed so far and gathered round us.

Before Albertine obeyed and took off her shoes, I would open her chemise. Her two little uplifted breasts were so round that they seemed not so much to be an integral part of her body as to have ripened there like fruit; and her belly (concealing the place where a man's is disfigured as though by an iron clamp left sticking in a statue that has been taken down from its niche) was closed, at the junction of her thighs, by two valves with a curve as languid, as reposeful, as cloistral as that of the horizon after the sun has set. She would take off her shoes, and lie down by my side.

O mighty attitudes of Man and Woman, in which there seeks to be united, in the innocence of the world's first days and with the humility of clay, what the Creation made separate, in which Eve is astonished and submissive before Man by whose side she awakens, as he himself, alone still, before God who has fashioned him! Albertine would fold her arms behind her dark hair, her hip swelling, her leg drooping with the inflexion of a swan's neck that stretches upwards and then curves back on itself. When she was lying completely on her side, there was a certain aspect of her face (so sweet and so beautiful from in front) which I could not endure, hook-nosed as in one of Leonardo's caricatures, seeming to betray the malice, the greed for gain, the deceitfulness of a spy whose presence in my house would have filled me with horror and whom that profile seemed to unmask. At once I took Albertine's face in my hands and altered its position.

'Be a good boy and promise me that if you don't come out tomorrow you'll work,' she would say as she slipped her chemise on again.

'Yes, but don't put on your dressing-gown yet.'

Sometimes I ended by falling asleep by her side. The room would grow cold, more wood would be wanted. I would try to find the bell above my head, but fail to do so, after fingering all the copper rods in turn save those between which it hung, and would say to Albertine who had sprung from the bed so that Françoise should not find us lying side by side: 'No, come back for a moment, I can't find the bell.'

Sweet, gay, innocent moments to all appearance, and yet moments in which there gathers the unsuspected possibility of disaster, which makes the amorous life the most precarious of all, that in which the unpredictable rain of sulphur and brimstone falls after the most radiant moments, whereupon, without having the heart or the will to draw a lesson from our misfortune, we set to work at once to rebuild upon the slopes of the crater from which nothing but catastrophe can emerge. I was as carefree as those who imagine their happiness will last. It is precisely because this tenderness has been necessary to give birth to pain—and will return moreover at intervals to calm it—that men can be sincere with each other, and even with themselves, when they pride themselves on a woman's lovingness, although, taking things all in all, at the heart of their intimacy there lurks continuously and secretly, unavowed to the rest of the world, or revealed unintentionally by questions and inquiries, a painful disquiet. But this could not have come to birth without the preliminary tenderness, which even afterwards is intermittently necessary to make the pain bearable and to avoid ruptures; and concealment of the secret hell that a life shared with the woman in question really is, to the point of parading an allegedly tender intimacy, expresses a genuine point of view, a universal process of cause and effect, one of the modes whereby the production of grief and pain is rendered possible.

IT NO LONGER surprised me that Albertine should be in the house, and would not be going out tomorrow except with myself or in the custody of Andrée. These habits of shared life, these broad lines by which my existence was demarcated and within which nobody might penetrate but Albertine, and also (in the future plan, of which I was still unaware, of my life to come, like the plan drawn up by an architect for monuments which will not be erected until long afterwards) the remoter lines, parallel to these and broader still, by which, like an isolated hermitage, the somewhat rigid and monotonous prescription of my future loves was adumbrated, had in reality been traced that night at Balbec when, in the little train, after Albertine had revealed to me who it was that had brought her up, I had decided at all costs to remove her from certain influences and to prevent her from straying out of my sight for some days. Day after day had gone by, and these habits had become mechanical, but, like those rites the meaning of which History seeks to discover, I could have said (though I would not have wished to say) to anybody who asked me to explain the meaning of this life of seclusion which I carried so far as no longer to go to the theatre, that its origin lay in the anxiety of an evening and my need to prove to myself, during the days that followed, that the girl of whose unfortunate childhood I had learned should have no possibility, whether she wished to or not, of exposing herself to similar temptations. I no longer thought, except very rarely, of these possibilities, but they were nevertheless to remain vaguely present in my consciousness. The fact that I was destroying them—or trying to do so—day by day was doubtless the reason why I took such pleasure in kissing those cheeks which were no more beautiful than many others; beneath any carnal attraction at all deep, there is the permanent possibility of danger.

I HAD PROMISED Albertine that, if I did not go out with her, I would settle down to work. But in the morning, just as if, taking advantage of our being asleep, the house had miraculously flown, I awoke in different weather beneath another clime. We do not begin to work as soon as we disembark in a strange country to the conditions of which we have to adapt ourselves. And each day was for me a different country. How could I even recognise my indolence itself, under the novel forms which it assumed? Sometimes, on days when the weather was beyond redemption, mere residence in the house, situated in the midst of a steady and continuous rain, had all the gliding ease, the soothing silence, the interest of a sea voyage; another time, on a bright day, to lie still in bed was to let the lights and shadows play around me as round a tree-trunk. Or yet again, at the first strokes of the bell of a neighbouring convent, rare as the early morning worshippers, barely whitening the dark sky with their hesitant hail-showers, melted and scattered by the warm breeze, I would discern one of those tempestuous, disordered, delightful days, when the roofs, soaked by an intermittent downpour and dried by a gust of wind or a ray of sunshine, let fall a gurgling raindrop and, as they wait for the wind to turn again, preen their iridescent pigeon's-breast slates in the momentary sunshine; one of those days filled with so many changes of weather, atmospheric incidents, storms, that the idle man does not feel that he has wasted them because he has been taking an interest in the activity which, in default of himself, the atmosphere, acting as it were in his stead, has displayed; days similar to those times of revolution or war which do not seem empty to the schoolboy playing truant, because by loitering outside the Law Courts or by reading the newspapers he has the illusion of deriving from the events that have occurred, failing the work which he has neglected, an intellectual profit and an excuse for his idleness; days, finally, to which one may compare those on which some exceptional crisis has occurred in one's life from which the man who has never done anything imagines that he will acquire industrious habits if it is happily resolved: for instance, the morning on which he sets out for a duel which is to be fought under particularly dangerous conditions, and he is suddenly made aware, at the moment when it is perhaps about to be taken from him, of the value of a life of which he might have made use to begin some important work, or merely to enjoy a few pleasures, and of which he has failed to make any use at all. 'If only I'm not killed,' he says to himself, 'how I shall settle down to work the very minute, and how I shall enjoy myself too!' Life has in fact suddenly acquired a higher value in his eyes, because he puts into life everything that it seems to him capable of giving, instead of the little that he normally demands of it. He sees it in the light of his desire, not as his experience has taught him that he was apt to make it, that is to say so tawdry. It has, at that moment, become filled with work, travel, mountain-climbing, all the splendid things which, he tells himself, the fatal outcome of the duel may render impossible, without thinking that they were already impossible before there was any question of a duel, owing to the bad habits which, even had there been no duel, would have persisted. He returns home without even a scratch, but he continues to find the same obstacles to pleasures, excursions, travel, to everything which for a moment he had feared that death would deprive him of; life is sufficient for that. As for work—exceptional circumstances having the effect of intensifying what previously existed in a man, work in the industrious, idleness in the lazy—he takes a holiday from it.

I followed his example, and did as I had always done since my first resolution to become a writer, which I had made long ago, but which seemed to me to date from yesterday, because I had regarded each intervening day as non-existent. I treated this day in a similar fashion, allowing its showers of rain and bursts of sunshine to pass without doing anything, and vowing that I would begin to work next day. But then I was no longer the same man beneath a cloudless sky; the golden note of the bells contained, like honey, not only light but the sensation of light (and also the sickly savour of preserved fruits, because at Combray it had often loitered like a wasp over our cleared dinner-table). On this day of dazzling sunshine, to remain until nightfall with my eyes shut was a thing permitted, customary, health-giving, pleasant, seasonable, like keeping the outside shutters closed against the heat. It was in such weather as this that at the beginning of my second visit to Balbec I used to hear the violins of the orchestra amid the blue-green surge of the rising tide. How much more fully did I possess Albertine today! There were days when the sound of a bell striking the hour bore upon the sphere of its sonority a plaque so spread with moisture or with light that it was like a transcription for the blind or, if you like, a musical interpretation of the charm of rain or the charm of sunlight. So much so that, at the moment, as I lay in bed with my eyes shut, I said to myself that everything is capable of transposition and that a universe that was exclusively audible might be as full of variety as the other. Travelling lazily upstream from day to day as in a boat, and seeing an endlessly changing succession of enchanted scenes appear before my eyes, scenes which I did not choose, which a moment earlier had been invisible to me, and which my memory presented to me one after another without my being free to choose them, I idly pursued over that smooth expanse my stroll in the sunshine.

Those morning concerts at Balbec were not long past. And yet, at that comparatively recent time, I had given but little thought to Albertine. Indeed, on the very first days after my arrival, I had not known that she was at Balbec. From whom then had I learned it? Oh, yes, from Aimé. It was a fine sunny day like this. The worthy Aimé! He was glad to see me again. But he does not like Albertine. Not everybody can like her. Yes, it was he who told me that she was at Balbec. But how did he know? Ah! he had met her, had thought that she was badly-behaved. At that moment, as I approached Aimé's story by a different facet from the one it had presented when he had told it to me, my thoughts, which hitherto had been sailing blissfully over these untroubled waters, exploded suddenly, as though they had struck an invisible and perilous mine, treacherously moored at this point in my memory. He had told me that he had met her, that he had thought her badly-behaved. What had he meant by bad behaviour? I had understood him to mean vulgar behaviour, because, to contradict him in advance, I had declared that she was most refined. But no, perhaps he had meant Gomorrhan behaviour. She was with another girl, perhaps their arms were round one another's waists, perhaps they were staring at other women, were indeed behaving in a manner which I had never seen Albertine adopt in my presence. Who was the other girl? Where had Aimé met her, this odious Albertine?

I tried to recall exactly what Aimé had said to me, in order to see whether it could be related to what I imagined, or whether he had meant nothing more than common manners. But in vain might I ask the question, the person who put it and the person who could supply the recollection were, alas, one and the same person, myself, who was momentarily duplicated but without any additional insight. Question as I might, it was myself who answered, I learned nothing more. I no longer gave a thought to Mlle Vinteuil. Born of a new suspicion, the fit of jealousy from which I was suffering was new too, or rather it was only the prolongation, the extension of that suspicion; it had the same theatre, which was no longer Montjouvain but the road upon which Aimé had met Albertine, and for its object one or other of the various friends who might have been with Albertine that day. It was perhaps a certain Elisabeth, or else perhaps those two girls whom Albertine had watched in the mirror at the Casino, while appearing not to see them. She had doubtless been having relations with them, and also with Esther, Bloch's cousin. Such relations, had they been revealed to me by a third person, would have been enough almost to kill me, but since it was I who imagined them, I took care to add sufficient uncertainty to deaden the pain. We succeed in absorbing daily in enormous doses, under the guise of suspicions, this same idea that we are being betrayed, a quite small quantity of which might prove fatal if injected by the needle of a shattering word. And it is no doubt for that reason, and as a by-product of the instinct of self-preservation, that the same jealous man does not hesitate to form the most terrible suspicions upon a basis of innocuous facts, provided that, whenever any proof is brought to him, he refuses to accept the irrefutable evidence. Besides, love is an incurable malady, like those diathetic states in which rheumatism affords the sufferer a brief respite only to be replaced by epileptiform headaches. If my jealous suspicion was calmed, I then felt a grudge against Albertine for not having been tender enough, perhaps for having made fun of me with Andrée. I thought with alarm of the idea that she must have formed if Andrée had repeated all our conversations; the future loomed black and menacing. This mood of depression left me only if a new jealous suspicion drove me to further inquiries or if, on the other hand, Albertine's displays of affection made my happiness seem to me insignificant. Who could this girl be? I must write to Aimé, try to see him, and then check his statement by talking to Albertine, making her confess. In the meantime, convinced that it must be Bloch's cousin, I asked Bloch himself, who had not the remotest idea of my purpose, simply to let me see her photograph, or, better still, to arrange for me to meet her.

How many persons, cities, roads jealousy makes us eager thus to know! It is a thirst for knowledge thanks to which, with regard to various isolated points, we end by acquiring every possible notion in turn except the one that we require. One can never tell whether a suspicion will not arise, for, all of a sudden, one recalls a remark that was not clear, an alibi that cannot have been given without a purpose. One has not seen the person again, but there is such a thing as a retrospective jealousy, that is born only after we have left the person, a delayed-action jealousy. Perhaps the habit that I had acquired of nursing within me certain desires, the desire for a young girl of good family such as those I used to see pass beneath my window escorted by their governesses, and especially for the girl whom Saint-Loup had mentioned to me, the one who frequented houses of ill fame, the desire for handsome lady's-maids, and especially for Mme Putbus's, the desire to go to the country in early spring to see once again hawthorns, apple-trees in blossom, storms, the desire for Venice, the desire to settle down to work, the desire to live like other people—perhaps the habit of storing up all these desires, without assuaging any of them, contenting myself with a promise to myself not to forget to satisfy them one

# How many persons, cities, roads jealousy makes us eager thus to know!

day—perhaps this habit, so many years old already, of perpetual postponement, of what M. de Charlus used to castigate under the name of procrastination, had become so prevalent in me that it took hold of my jealous suspicions also and, while encouraging me to make a mental note that I would not fail, some day, to have things out with Albertine as regards the girl, or possibly girls (this part of the story was confused and blurred in my memory and to all intents and purposes indecipherable) with whom Aimé had met her, made me also postpone this inquest. In any case, I would not mention the subject to my mistress this evening, for fear of making her think me jealous and so offending her.

And yet when, on the following day, Bloch sent me the photograph of his cousin Esther, I made haste to forward it to Aimé. And at the same moment I remembered that Albertine had that morning refused me a pleasure which might indeed have tired her. Was that in order to reserve it for someone else, this afternoon, perhaps? For whom? Jealousy is thus endless, for even if the beloved, by dying for instance, can no longer provoke it by her actions, it may happen that memories subsequent to any event suddenly materialise and behave in our minds as though they too were events, memories which hitherto we had never explored, which had seemed to us unimportant, and to which our own reflexion upon them is sufficient, without any external factors, to give a new and terrible meaning. There is no need for there to be two of you, it is enough to be alone in your room, thinking, for fresh betrayals by your mistress to come to light, even though she is dead. And so we ought not to fear in love, as in everyday life, the future alone, but even the past, which often comes to life for us only when the future has come and gone—and not only the past which we discover after the event but the past which we have long kept stored within ourselves and suddenly learn how to interpret.

No matter, I was only too happy, as afternoon turned to evening, that the hour was not far off when I should be able to look to Albertine's presence for the appeasement which I needed. Unfortunately, the evening that followed was one of those when this appeasement was not forthcoming, when the kiss that Albertine would give me when she left me for the night, very different from her usual kiss, would no more soothe me than my mother's kiss had soothed me long ago, on days when she was vexed with me and I dared not call her back although I knew that I should be unable to sleep. Such evenings were now those on which Albertine had formed for the next day some plan about which she did not wish me to know. Had she confided it to me, I would have shown an eagerness to ensure its realisation that no one but Albertine could have inspired in me. But she told me nothing, and she had no need to tell me anything; as soon as she came in, before she had even crossed the threshold of my room, while she was still wearing her hat or toque, I had already detected the unknown, restive, desperate, uncontrollable desire. These were often the

evenings when I had awaited her return with the most loving thoughts, and looked forward to throwing my arms
round her neck with the warmest affection. Alas, misun-
derstandings such as I had often had with my parents,
whom I would find cold or irritable when I ran to embrace
them, overflowing with love, are as nothing in comparison
with those that occur between lovers. The anguish then is
far less superficial, far harder to endure; it has its seat in a
deeper layer of the heart.

On this particular evening, however, Albertine was
obliged to mention the plan that she had in mind; I gathered at once that she wished to go next day to pay a visit to
Mme Verdurin, a visit to which in itself I would have seen
no objection. But evidently her object was to meet someone there, to prepare some future pleasure. Otherwise she
would not have attached so much importance to this visit.
That is to say, she would not have kept on assuring me that
it was of no importance. I had in the course of my life followed a progression which was the opposite of that
adopted by peoples who make use of phonetic writing only
after having considered the characters as a set of symbols;
having, for so many years, looked for the real life and
thought of other people only in the direct statements
about them which they supplied me with of their own free
will, in the absence of these I had come to attach importance, on the contrary, only to disclosures that are not a
rational and analytical expression of the truth; the words
themselves did not enlighten me unless they were

interpreted in the same way as a rush of blood to the cheeks of a person who is embarrassed, or as a sudden silence. Such and such an adverb (for instance that used by M. de Cambremer when he understood that I was 'literary' and, not having yet spoken to me, as he was describing a visit he had paid to the Verdurins, turned to me with: '*Incidentally*, Borelli was there!') bursting into flames through the involuntary, sometimes perilous contact of two ideas which the speaker has not expressed but which, by applying the appropriate methods of analysis or electrolysis, I was able to extract from it, told me more than a long speech. Albertine sometimes let fall in her conversation one or other of these precious amalgams which I made haste to 'treat' so as to transform them into lucid ideas.

It is in fact one of the most terrible things for the lover that whereas particular details—which only experiment or espionage, among so many possible realisations, would ever make known to him—are so difficult to discover, the truth on the other hand is so easy to detect or merely to sense. Often, at Balbec, I had seen her fasten on girls who came past us a sudden lingering stare, like a physical contact, after which, if I knew the girls, she would say to me: 'Suppose we asked them to join us? I should so enjoy insulting them.' And now, for some time past, doubtless since she had succeeded in reading my mind, no request to me to invite anyone, not a word, not even a sidelong glance from her eyes, which had become objectless and mute, and, with the abstracted, vacant expression that

accompanied them, as revealing as had been their mag-
netic swerve before. Yet it was impossible for me to
reproach her, or to ply her with questions about things
which she would have declared to be so petty, so trivial,
stored up by me simply for the pleasure of 'nit-picking.' It
is hard enough to say: 'Why did you stare at that girl who
went past?' but a great deal harder to say: 'Why did you not
stare at her?' And yet I knew quite well—or at least I should
have known if I had not chosen instead to believe those
affirmations of hers—what Albertine's demeanour com-
prehended and proved, like such and such a contradiction
in the course of conversation which often I did not perceive until long after I had left her, which kept me in
anguish all night long, which I never dared mention to her
again, but which nevertheless continued to honour my
memory from time to time with its periodical visits. Even
in the case of these furtive or sidelong glances on the
beach at Balbec or in the streets of Paris, I might sometimes wonder whether the person who provoked them was
not only an object of desire at the moment when she
passed, but an old acquaintance, or else some girl who had
simply been mentioned to her and whom, when I heard
about it, I was astonished that anybody could have mentioned to her, so remote was she from what one would
have guessed Albertine's range of acquaintance to be. But
the Gomorrah of today is a jigsaw puzzle made up of pieces
that come from places where one least expected to find
them. Thus I once saw at Rivebelle a big dinner-party of

ten women, all of whom I happened to know, at least by name, and who, though as dissimilar as could be, were none the less perfectly united, so much so that I never saw a party so homogeneous, albeit so composite.

To return to the girls whom we passed in the street, never would Albertine stare at an old person, man or woman, with such fixity, or on the other hand with such reserve and as though she saw nothing. Cuckolded husbands who know nothing in fact know perfectly well. But it requires more accurate and abundant evidence to create a scene of jealousy. Besides, if jealousy helps us to discover a certain tendency to falsehood in the woman we love, it multiplies this tendency a hundredfold when the woman has discovered that we are jealous. She lies (to an extent to which she has never lied to us before), whether from pity, or from fear, or because she instinctively shies away in a flight that is symmetrical with our investigations. True, there are love affairs in which from the start a woman of easy virtue has posed as virtue incarnate in the eyes of the man who is in love with her. But how many others consist of two diametrically opposite periods! In the first, the woman speaks almost freely, with slight modifications, of her zest for pleasure and of the amorous life which it has made her lead, all of which she will deny later on with the utmost vigour to the same man when she senses that he is jealous of her and spying on her. He comes to regret the days of those first confidences, the memory of which torments him nevertheless. If the woman continued to make them, she would furnish him almost unaided with the secret of her conduct which he has been vainly pursuing day after day. And besides, what abandon those early confidences proved, what trust, what friendship! If she cannot live without being unfaithful to him, at least she would be doing so as a friend, telling him of her pleasures, associating him with them. And he thinks with regret of the sort of life which the early stages of their love seemed to promise, which the sequel has rendered impossible, turning that love into something agonisingly painful, which will make a final parting, according to circumstances, either inevitable or impossible.

Sometimes the script from which I deciphered Albertine's lies, without being ideographic, needed simply to be read backwards; thus this evening she had tossed at me casually the message, intended to pass almost unnoticed: 'I may go and see the Verdurins tomorrow. I don't really know whether I will go, I don't particularly want to.' A childish anagram of the admission: 'I shall go to the Verdurins' tomorrow, it's absolutely certain, I attach the utmost importance to it.' This apparent hesitation indicated a firm resolution and was intended to diminish the importance of the visit while informing me of it. Albertine always adopted a dubitative tone for irrevocable decisions. Mine was no less irrevocable: I would see that this visit to Mme Verdurin did not take place. Jealousy is often only an anxious need to be tyrannical applied to matters of love. I had doubtless inherited from my father this abrupt,

arbitrary desire to threaten the people I loved best in the
hopes with which they were lulling themselves with a
sense of security which I wanted to expose to them as
false; when I saw that Albertine had planned without my
knowledge, behind my back, an expedition which I would
have done everything in the world to make easier and
more pleasant for her had she taken me into her confi-
dence, I said casually, in order to make her tremble, that I
expected to go out the next day myself.

I began to suggest to Albertine other expeditions in
directions which would have made the visit to the Verdurins impossible, in words stamped with a feigned
indifference beneath which I strove to conceal my agitation. But she had detected it. It encountered in her the
electric power of a contrary will which violently repulsed
it; I could see the sparks flash from Albertine's pupils.
What use was it, though, to pay attention to what her eyes
were saying at that moment? How had I failed to observe
long ago that Albertine's eyes belonged to the category
which even in a quite ordinary person seems to be composed of a number of fragments because of all the places
in which the person wishes to be—and to conceal the
desire to be—on that particular day? Eyes mendaciously
kept always immobile and passive, but none the less
dynamic, measurable in the yards or miles to be tra-
versed before they reach the desired, the implacably
desired meeting-place, eyes that are not so much smiling
at the pleasure which tempts them as shadowed with

melancholy and discouragement because there may be a difficulty in their getting there. Even when you hold them in your hands, such persons are fugitives. To understand the emotions which they arouse, and which others, even better-looking, do not, we must recognise that they are not immobile but in motion, and add to their person a sign corresponding to that which in physics denotes speed.

If you upset their plans for the day, they confess to you the pleasure they had concealed from you: 'I did so want to go and have tea with so and so who I'm fond of.' And then, six months later, if you come to know the person in question, you will learn that the girl whose plans you had upset, who, trapped, in order that you might set her free had confessed to you that she was thus in the habit of taking tea with a dear friend every day at the hour at which you did not see her, has never once been inside this person's house, that they have never had tea together, since the girl used to explain that her whole time was taken up by none other than yourself. And so the person with whom she confessed that she was going to tea, with whom she begged you to allow her to go to tea, that person, a reason admitted by necessity, it was not her, it was somebody else, it was something else still! What something else? Which somebody else?

Alas, the multifaceted eyes, far-ranging and melancholy, might enable us perhaps to measure distance, but do not indicate direction. The boundless field of possibilities extends before us, and if by any chance the reality presented itself to our eyes, it would be so far outside the limits of the possible that, knocking suddenly against this looming wall, we should fall over backwards in a daze. It is not even essential that we should have proof of her movement and flight, it is enough that we should guess them. She had promised us a letter; we were calm, we were no longer in love. The letter has not come; each mail fails to bring it; what can have happened? Anxiety is born afresh, and love. It is such people more than any others who inspire love in us, to our desolation. For every new anxiety that we feel on their account strips them in our eyes of some of their personality. We were resigned to suffering, thinking that we loved outside ourselves, and we perceive that our love is a function of our sorrow, that our love perhaps is our sorrow, and that its object is only to a very small extent the girl with the raven hair. But, when all is said, it is such people more than any others who inspire love.

More often than not, a body becomes the object of love only when an emotion, fear of losing it, uncertainty of getting it back, melts into it. Now this sort of anxiety has a great affinity for bodies. It adds to them a quality which surpasses beauty itself, which is one of the reasons why we see men who are indifferent to the most beautiful women fall passionately in love with others who appear to us ugly. To such beings, such fugitive beings, their own nature and our anxiety fasten wings. And even when they are with us the look in their eyes seems to warn us that they are about to take flight. The proof of this beauty, surpassing beauty itself, that wings add is that often, for us, the same person is alternately winged and wingless. Afraid of losing her, we forget all the others. Sure of keeping her, we compare her with those others whom at once we prefer to her. And as these fears and these certainties may vary from week to week, a person may one week see everything that gave us pleasure sacrificed to her, in the following week be sacrificed herself, and so on for months on end. All of which would be incomprehensible did we not know (from the experience, which every man shares, of having at least once in a lifetime ceased to love a woman, forgotten her) how very insignificant in herself a woman is when she is no longer—or is not yet—permeable to our emotions. And, of course, if we speak of fugitive beings it is equally true of imprisoned ones, of captive women whom we think we shall never be able to possess. Hence men detest procuresses, because they facilitate flight and dangle temptations, but if on the other hand we are in love with a cloistered woman, we willingly have recourse to a procuress to snatch her from her prison and bring her to us. In so far as relations with women whom we abduct are less permanent than others, the reason is that the fear of not succeeding in procuring them or the dread of seeing them escape is the whole of our love for them and that once they have been carried off from their husbands, torn from their footlights, cured of the temptation to leave us, dissociated in short from our emotion whatever it may be, they are only themselves, that is to say next to nothing, and, so long desired, are soon forsaken by the very man who was so afraid of their forsaking him.

I have said: 'How could I have failed to guess?' But had I not guessed it from the first day at Balbec? Had I not detected in Albertine one of those girls beneath whose envelope of flesh more hidden persons stir, I will not say than in a pack of cards still in its box, a closed cathedral or a theatre before we enter it, but than in the whole vast ever-changing crowd? Not only all these persons, but the desire, the voluptuous memory, the restless searching of so many persons. At Balbec I had not been troubled because I had never even supposed that one day I should be following a trail, even a false trail. Nevertheless, it had given Albertine, in my eyes, the plenitude of someone filled to the brim by the superimposition of so many persons, of so many desires and voluptuous memories of persons. And now that she had one day let fall the name 'Mlle Vinteuil,' I should have liked, not to tear off her dress to see her body, but through her body to see and read the whole diary of her memories and her future passionate assignations.

Strange how the things that are probably most insignificant suddenly assume an extraordinary value when a person whom we love (or who has lacked only this duplicity to make us love her) conceals them from us! In itself, suffering does not of necessity inspire in us sentiments of love or hatred towards the person who causes it: a surgeon can hurt us without arousing any personal emotion in us. But with a woman who has continued for some time to assure us that we are everything in the world to her, without being herself everything in the world to us, a woman whom we enjoy seeing, kissing, taking on our knee, we are astonished if we merely sense from a sudden resistance that she is not at our entire disposal. Disappointment may then revive in us the forgotten memory of an old anguish, which we nevertheless know to have been provoked not by this woman but by others whose betrayals stretch back like milestones through our past. And indeed, how have we the heart to go on living, how can we move a finger to preserve ourselves from death, in a world in which love is provoked only by lies and consists solely in our need to see our sufferings appeased by the person who has made us suffer? To escape from the depths of despondency that follow the discovery of this lying and this resistance, there is the sad remedy of endeavouring to act, against her will, with the help of people whom we feel to be more closely involved than we are in her life, upon her who is resisting us and lying to us, to play the cheat in turn, to make ourselves loathed. But the suffering caused by such a love is of the kind which must inevitably lead the sufferer to seek an illusory comfort in a change of position. These means of action are not wanting, alas! And the horror of the kind of love which anxiety alone has engendered lies in the fact that we turn over and over incessantly in our cage the most trivial utterances; not to mention that rarely do the people for whom we feel this love appeal to us physically to any great extent, since it is not our deliberate preference, but the accident of a moment's anguish (a moment indefinitely prolonged by our weakness of character, which repeats its experiments every evening until it yields to sedatives) that has chosen for us.

No doubt my love for Albertine was not the most barren of those to which, through lack of will-power, a man may descend, for it was not entirely platonic; she did give me some carnal satisfaction, and moreover she was intelligent. But all this was supererogatory. What occupied my mind was not something intelligent that she might have said, but a chance remark that had aroused in me a doubt as to her actions; I tried to remember whether she had said this or that, in what tone, at what moment, in response to what words, to reconstruct the whole scene of her dialogue with me, to recall at what moment she had expressed a desire to visit the Verdurins, what word of mine had brought that look of vexation to her face. The most important event might have been at issue without my going to so much trouble to establish the truth of it, to reconstitute its precise atmosphere and colour. No doubt, after these anxieties have intensified to a degree which we find unbearable, we sometimes manage to calm them altogether for an evening. We too are invited to the party which the woman we love was to attend and the true nature of which has been obsessing us for days; she has neither looks nor words for anyone but us; we take her home and then, all our anxieties dispelled, we enjoy a repose as complete and as healing as the deep sleep that comes after a long walk. And no doubt such repose is worth a high price. But would it not have been simpler not to buy ourselves, deliberately, the preceding anxiety, and at an even higher price? Besides, we know all too well that however profound these temporary respites may be, anxiety will still prevail. Often, indeed, it is revived by a remark that was intended to set our mind at rest. The demands of our jealousy and the blindness of our credulity are greater than the woman we love could ever suppose. When, spontaneously, she swears to us that such and such a man is no more to her than a friend, she shatters us by informing us—something we never suspected—that he has been her friend. While she is telling us, in proof of her sincerity, how they had tea together that very afternoon, at each word that she utters the invisible, the unsuspected, takes shape before our eyes. She admits that he has asked her to be his mistress, and we suffer agonies at the thought that she can have listened to his overtures. She refused them, she says. But presently, when we recall her story, we wonder whether that refusal is really genuine, for there is wanting, between the different things that she said to us, that logical and necessary connexion which, more than the facts related, is the sign of truth. Besides, there was that frightening note of scorn in her voice: 'I said to him no, categorically,' which is to be found in every class of society when a woman is lying. We must nevertheless thank her for having refused, encourage

**The demands of our jealousy and the blindness of our credulity are greater than the woman we love could ever suppose**

her by our kindness to repeat these painful confidences in the future. At the most, we may remark: 'But if he had already made advances to you, why did you accept his invitation to tea?' 'So that he should not hold it against me and say that I hadn't been nice to him.' And we dare not reply that by refusing she would perhaps have been nicer to us.

Albertine alarmed me further when she said that I was quite right to say, out of regard for her reputation, that I was not her lover, since 'for that matter,' she went on, 'it's perfectly true that you aren't.' I was not perhaps her lover in the full sense of the word, but then, was I to suppose that all the things that we did together she did also with all the other men whose mistress she swore to me that she had never been? The desire to know at all costs what Albertine was thinking, whom she saw, whom she loved—how strange that I should sacrifice everything to this need, since I had felt the same need to know in the case of Gilberte names and facts which now meant nothing to me! I was perfectly well aware that in themselves Albertine's actions were of no greater interest. It is curious that a first love, if by the fragile state in which it leaves one's heart it paves the way for subsequent loves, does not at least provide one, in view of the identity of symptoms and sufferings, with the means of curing them. Besides, is there any need to know a fact? Are we not aware beforehand, in a general way, of the mendacity and even the discretion of those women who have something to conceal? Is there any possibility of error? They make a virtue of their silence, when we would give anything to make them speak. And we feel certain that they have assured their accomplice: 'I never say anything. It won't be through me that anybody will hear about it, I never say anything.'

A man may give his fortune and even his life for a woman, and yet know quite well that in ten years' time, more or less, he would refuse her the fortune, prefer to keep his life. For then that woman would be detached from him, alone, that is to say non-existent. What attaches us to people are the countless roots, the innumerable threads which are our memories of last night, our hopes for tomorrow morning, the continuous weft of habit from which we can never free ourselves. Just as there are misers who hoard from generosity, so we are spendthrifts who spend from avarice, and it is not so much to a person that we sacrifice our life as to everything of ours that may have become attached to that person, all those hours and days, all those things compared with which the life we have not yet lived, our life in the relative future, seems to us more remote, more detached, less intimate, less our own. What we need is to extricate ourselves from these bonds which are so much more important than the person, but they have the effect of creating in us temporary obligations which mean that we dare not leave the person for fear of being badly thought of, whereas later on we would so dare, for, detached from us, that person would no longer be part of us, and because in reality we create obligations (even if, by an apparent contradiction, they should lead to suicide) towards ourselves alone.

If I was not in love with Albertine (and of this I could not be sure) then there was nothing extraordinary in the place that she occupied in my life: we live only with what we do not love, with what we have brought to live with us only in order to kill the intolerable love, whether it be for a woman, for a place, or again for a woman embodying a place. Indeed we should be terrified of beginning to love again if a new separation were to occur. I had not yet reached this stage with Albertine. Her lies, her admissions, left me to complete the task of elucidating the truth: her innumerable lies, because she was not content with merely lying, like everyone who imagines that he or she is loved, but was by nature, quite apart from this, a liar (and so inconsistent moreover that, even if she told me the truth every time about, for instance, what she thought of other people, she would say something different every time); her admissions, because, being so rare, so quickly cut short, they left between them, in so far as they concerned the past, huge blanks over the whole expanse of which I was obliged to retrace—and for that first of all to discover—her life.

As for the present, so far as I could interpret the sibylline utterances of Françoise, it was not only on particular points but over a whole area that Albertine lied to me, and 'one fine day' I would see what Françoise pretended to know, what she refused to tell me, what I dared not ask her.

It was no doubt with the same jealousy that she had shown in the past with regard to Eulalie that Françoise would speak of the most unlikely things, but so vaguely that at most one could deduce therefrom the highly improbable insinuation that the poor captive (who was a lover of women) preferred marriage with somebody who did not appear to be me. If this had been so, how, in spite of her telepathic powers, could Françoise have come to hear of it? Certainly, Albertine's statements could give me no definite enlightenment, for they were as different day by day as the colours of a spinning-top that has almost come to a standstill. However, it seemed that it was hatred more than anything else that impelled Françoise to speak. Not a day went by without her addressing to me, and I in my mother's absence enduring, such speeches as:

'To be sure, you're very nice, and I shall never forget the debt of gratitude that I owe you' (this probably so that I might establish fresh claims upon her gratitude) 'but the house has become infected ever since niceness brought in deceitfulness, ever since cleverness has been protecting the stupidest person that ever was seen, ever since refinement, good manners, wit, dignity in all things, the appearance and the reality of a prince, allow themselves to be dictated to and plotted against and me to be humiliated—me who've been forty years in the family—by vice, by everything that's most vulgar and base.'

What Françoise resented most about Albertine was having to take orders from somebody who was not one of

ourselves, and also the strain of the additional housework
which, affecting the health of our old servant (who would
not, for all that, accept any help in the house, not being a
'good for nothing'), in itself would have accounted for her
irritability and her furious hatred. Certainly, she would
have liked to see Albertine-Esther banished from the
house. This was Françoise's dearest wish. And, by consol-
ing her, its fulfilment would in itself have given our old
servant some rest. But to my mind there was more to it
than this. So violent a hatred could have originated only in
an over-strained body. And, more even than of consider-
ation, Françoise was in need of sleep.

ALBERTINE WENT TO take off her things and, to lose no
time in finding out what I wanted to know, I seized the
telephone receiver and invoked the implacable deities, but
succeeded only in arousing their fury which expressed
itself in the single word 'Engaged.' Andrée was in fact
engaged in talking to someone else. As I waited for her to
finish her conversation, I wondered why it was—now that
so many of our painters are seeking to revive the feminine
portraits of the eighteenth century, in which the cleverly
devised setting is a pretext for portraying expressions of
expectation, sulkiness, interest, reverie—why it was that
none of our modern Bouchers or Fragonards had yet
painted, instead of 'The Letter' or 'The Harpsichord,' this
scene which might be entitled 'At the telephone,' in which
there would come spontaneously to the lips of the listener

a smile that is all the more genuine because it is conscious of being unobserved.

Finally I got through to Andrée: 'Are you coming to call for Albertine tomorrow?' I asked, and as I uttered Albertine's name, I thought of the envy Swann had aroused in me when he had said to me, on the day of the Princesse de Guermantes's party: 'Come and see Odette,' and I had thought how potent, when all was said, was a Christian name which, in the eyes of the whole world including Odette herself, had on Swann's lips alone this entirely possessive sense. Such a monopoly—summed up in a single word—over the whole existence of another person had appeared to me, whenever I was in love, to be sweet indeed! But in fact, when we are in a position to say it, either we no longer care, or else habit, while not blunting its tenderness, has changed its sweetness to bitterness. I knew that I alone was in a position to say 'Albertine' in that tone to Andrée. And yet, to Albertine, to Andrée, and to myself, I felt that I was nothing. And I realised the impossibility which love comes up against. We imagine that it has as its object a being that can be laid down in front of us, enclosed within a body. Alas, it is the extension of that being to all the points in space and time that it has occupied and will occupy. If we do not possess its contact with this or that place, this or that hour, we do not possess that being. But we cannot touch all these points. If only they were indicated to us, we might perhaps contrive to reach out to them. But we grope for them without finding them.

Hence mistrust, jealousy, persecutions. We waste precious time on absurd clues and pass by the truth without suspecting it.

But already one of the irascible deities with the breath-takingly agile handmaidens was becoming irritated, not because I was speaking but because I was saying nothing.

'Come along, I've been holding the line for you all this time; I shall cut you off.'

However, she did nothing of the sort but, evoking Andrée's presence, enveloped it, like the great poet that a damsel of the telephone always is, in the atmosphere peculiar to the home, the district, the very life itself of Albertine's friend.

'Is that you?' asked Andrée, whose voice was projected towards me with an instantaneous speed by the goddess whose privilege it is to make sound more swift than light.

'Listen,' I replied, 'go wherever you like, anywhere, except to Mme Verdurin's. You must at all cost keep Albertine away from there tomorrow.'

'But that's just where she's supposed to be going.'

'Ah!'

But I was obliged to break off the conversation for a moment and to make menacing gestures, for if Françoise continued—as though it were something as unpleasant as vaccination or as dangerous as the aeroplane—to refuse to learn to use the telephone, whereby she would have spared us the trouble of conversations which she might intercept without any harm, on the other hand she would at once come into the room whenever I was engaged in a conversation so private that I was particularly anxious to keep it from her ears. When she had left the room at last, not without lingering to take away various objects that had been lying there since the previous day and might perfectly well have been left there for an hour longer, and to put on to the fire a log made quite superfluous by the burning heat generated in me by the intruder's presence and my fear of finding myself 'cut off' by the operator, 'I'm sorry,' I said to Andrée, 'I was interrupted. Is it absolutely certain that she has to go to the Verdurins' tomorrow?'

'Absolutely, but I can tell her that you don't want her to.'

'No, not at all, but I might possibly come with you.'

'Ah!' said Andrée, in a voice that sounded annoyed and somehow alarmed by my audacity, which was incidentally fortified as a result.

'Well then, good-night, and please forgive me for disturbing you for nothing.'

'Not at all,' said Andrée, and (since, now that the telephone has come into general use, a decorative ritual of polite phrases has grown up round it, as round the tea-tables of the past) she added: 'It's been a great pleasure to hear your voice.'

I might have said the same, and with greater truth than Andrée, for I had been deeply affected by the sound of her voice, having never noticed before that it was so different from the voices of other people. Then I recalled other voices still, women's voices especially, some of them slowed down by the precision of a question and by mental concentration, others made breathless, even interrupted at moments, by the lyrical flow of what they were relating; I recalled one by one the voices of all the girls I had known at Balbec, then Gilberte's, then my grandmother's, then Mme de Guermantes's; I found them all dissimilar, moulded by a speech peculiar to each of them, each playing on a different instrument, and I thought to myself how thin must be the concert performed in paradise by the three or four angel musicians of the old painters, when I saw, mounting to the throne of God by tens, by hundreds, by thousands, the harmonious and multiphonic salutation of all the Voices. I did not leave the telephone without thanking, in a few propitiatory words, the goddess who reigns over the speed of sound for having kindly exercised on behalf of my humble words a power which made them a hundred times more rapid than thunder. But my thanksgiving received no other response than that of being cut off.

When Albertine came back to my room, she was wearing a black satin dress which had the effect of making her seem paler, of turning her into the pallid, intense Parisian woman, etiolated by lack of fresh air, by the atmosphere of crowds and perhaps by the practice of vice, whose eyes seemed the more uneasy because they were not brightened by any colour in her cheeks.

'Guess,' I said to her, 'who I've just been talking to on the telephone. Andrée!'

'Andrée?' exclaimed Albertine in a loud, astonished, excited voice that so simple a piece of intelligence hardly seemed to call for. 'I hope she remembered to tell you that we met Mme Verdurin the other day.'

'Mme Verdurin? I don't remember,' I replied as though I were thinking of something else, in order to appear indifferent to this meeting and not to betray Andrée who had told me where Albertine was going next day. But how could I tell whether Andrée was not herself betraying me, whether she would not tell Albertine tomorrow that I had asked her to prevent her at all costs from going to the Verdurins', and whether she had not already revealed to her that I had on several occasions made similar recommendations? She had assured me that she had never repeated anything, but the value of this assertion was counterbalanced in my mind by the impression that for some time past Albertine's face had ceased to show the trust that she had placed in me for so long.

Suffering, when we are in love, ceases from time to time, but only to resume in a different form. We weep to see the beloved no longer respond to us with those bursts of affection, those amorous advances of earlier days; we suffer even more when, having relinquished them with us, she resumes them with others; then, from this suffering, we are distracted by a new and still more agonising pang, the suspicion that she has lied to us about how she spent the previous evening, when she was no doubt unfaithful to us; this suspicion in turn is dispelled, and we

are soothed by our mistress's affectionate kindness; but
then a forgotten word comes back to us; we had been told
that she was ardent in moments of pleasure, whereas we
have always found her calm; we try to picture to ourselves
these passionate frenzies with others, we feel how very
little we are to her, we observe an air of boredom, longing,
melancholy while we are talking, we observe like a black
sky the slovenly clothes she puts on when she is with us,
keeping for other people the dresses with which she used
to flatter us. If, on the contrary, she is affectionate, what
joy for a moment! But when we see that little tongue stuck
out as though in invitation, we think of those to whom that
invitation was so often addressed that even perhaps with
me, without her thinking of those others, it had remained
for Albertine, by force of long habit, an automatic signal.
Then the feeling that she is bored by us returns. But suddenly this pain is reduced to nothing when we think of the
unknown evil element in her life, of the places, impossible
to identify, where she has been, where she still goes perhaps during the hours when we are not with her, if indeed
she is not planning to live there altogether, those places in
which she is separated from us, does not belong to us, is
happier than when she is with us. Such are the revolving
searchlights of jealousy.

Jealousy is moreover a demon that cannot be exorcised,
but constantly reappears in new incarnations. Even if we
could succeed in exterminating them all, in keeping the
beloved for ever, the Spirit of Evil would then adopt

But when we see that little tongue stuck out as though in invitation, we think of those to whom that invitation was so often addressed another form, more pathetic still, despair at having obtained fidelity only by force, despair at not being loved.

Tender and sweet though Albertine was on certain evenings, she no longer had any of those spontaneous impulses which I remembered from Balbec when she used to say 'How very nice you are, really!' and her whole heart seemed to go out to me unrestrained by any of those grievances which she now felt and which she kept to herself because she doubtless considered them irremediable, impossible to forget, unavowable, but which nevertheless created between us a significant verbal prudence on her part or an impassable barrier of silence.

'And may one be allowed to know why you telephoned to Andrée?'

'To ask whether she had any objection to my joining you tomorrow and paying the Verdurins the visit I've been promising them since La Raspelière.'

'Just as you like. But I warn you, there's an appalling fog this evening, and it's sure to last over tomorrow. I mention it because I shouldn't like you to make yourself ill. Personally, I need hardly say that I'd love you to come with us. However,' she added with a thoughtful air, 'I'm not at all sure that I'll go to the Verdurins'. They've been so kind to me that I ought, really . . . Next to you, they've been nicer to me than anybody, but there are some things about them that I don't quite like. I simply must go to the Bon Marché or the Trois-Quartiers and get a white bodice to wear with this dress which is really too black.'

To allow Albertine to go by herself into a big shop crowded with people perpetually brushing against one, provided with so many exits that a woman can always say that when she came out she could not find her carriage which was waiting further along the street, was something that I was quite determined never to consent to, but the thought of it made me extremely unhappy. And yet it did not occur to me that I ought long ago to have ceased to see Albertine, for she had entered, for me, upon that lamentable period in which a person, scattered in space and time, is no longer a woman but a series of events on which we can throw no light, a series of insoluble problems, a sea which, like Xerxes, we scourge with rods in an absurd attempt to punish it for what it has engulfed. Once this period has begun, we are perforce vanquished. Happy are they who understand this in time not to prolong unduly a futile, exhausting struggle, hemmed in on every side by the limits of the imagination, a struggle in which jealousy plays so sorry a part that the same man who, once upon a time, if the eyes of the woman who was always by his side rested for an instant upon another man, imagined an intrigue and suffered endless torments, now resigns himself to allowing her to go out by herself, sometimes with the man whom he knows to be her lover, preferring to the unknowable this torture which at least he knows! It is a question of the rhythm to be adopted, which afterwards one follows from force of habit. Neurotics who could never stay away from a dinner-party will eventually take rest cures which never seem to them to last long enough; women who recently were still of easy virtue live in penitence. Jealous lovers who, to keep an eye on the woman they loved, cut short their hours of sleep, deprived themselves of rest, now feeling that her desires, the world so vast and secret, and time are too much for them, allow her to go out without them, then to travel, and finally separate from her. Jealousy thus perishes for want of nourishment and has survived so long only by clamouring incessantly for fresh food. I was still a long way from this state.

I was now at liberty to go out with Albertine as often as I wished. As there had recently sprung up round Paris a number of aerodromes, which are to aeroplanes what harbours are to ships, and as, ever since the day when, on the way to La Raspelière, that almost mythological encounter with an airman, at whose passage overhead my horse had reared, had been to me like a symbol of liberty, I often chose to end our day's excursion—with the ready approval of Albertine, a passionate lover of every form of sport—at one of these aerodromes. We went there, she and I, attracted by that incessant stir of departure and arrival which gives so much charm to a stroll along a jetty, or merely along a beach, to those who love the sea, and to loitering about an 'aviation centre' to those who love the sky. From time to time, amid the repose of the machines that lay inert and as though at anchor, we would see one being laboriously pulled by a number of mechanics, as a boat is dragged across the sand at the bidding of a tourist who wishes to go for an outing on the sea. Then the engine was started, the machine ran along the ground, gathered speed, until finally, all of a sudden, at right angles, it rose slowly, in the braced and as it were static ecstasy of a horizontal speed suddenly transformed into a majestic, vertical ascent. Albertine could not contain her joy, and would demand explanations of the mechanics who, now that the machine was in the air, were strolling back to the sheds. The passenger, meanwhile, was covering mile after mile; the huge skiff, upon which our eyes remained fixed, was now no more than a barely visible dot in the sky, a dot which, however, would gradually recover its solidity, its size, its volume, when, as the time allowed for the excursion drew to an end, the moment came for landing. And we watched with envy, Albertine and I, as he sprang to earth, the passenger who had gone up like that to enjoy in the solitary expanses of the open sky the calm and limpidity of evening. Then, whether from the aerodrome or from some museum or church that we had been visiting, we would return home together for dinner. And yet I did not return home calmed, as I used to be at Balbec by less frequent excursions which I rejoiced to see extend over a whole afternoon and would afterwards contemplate, standing out like clustering flowers, against the rest of Albertine's life as against an empty sky beneath which one muses pleasantly, without thinking. Albertine's time did not belong to me then in such ample quantities as today. Yet it had seemed to me then to belong to me much more, because I then took into account—my love rejoicing in them as in the bestowal of a favour—only the hours that she spent with me, whereas now—my jealousy searching anxiously among them for the possibility of a betrayal—it was only those hours that she spent apart from me.

Tomorrow, evidently, she was looking forward to a few such hours. I must choose to cease from suffering or to cease from loving. For, just as in the beginning it is formed by desire, so afterwards love is kept in existence only by painful anxiety. I felt that part of Albertine's life eluded me. Love, in the pain of anxiety as in the bliss of desire, is a demand for a whole. It is born, and it survives, only if some part remains for it to conquer. We love only what we do not wholly possess. Albertine was lying when she told me that she probably would not go to see the Verdurins, as I was lying when I said that I wished to go. She was seeking merely to dissuade me from going out with her, and I, by my abrupt announcement of this plan which I had no intention of putting into practice, to touch what I felt to be her most sensitive spot, to track down the desire that she was concealing and to force her to admit that my company next day would prevent her from gratifying it. She had virtually made this admission by ceasing suddenly to wish to go to see the Verdurins.

'If you don't want to go to the Verdurins',' I told her, 'there is a splendid charity show at the Trocadéro.' She listened to my exhortations to attend it with a doleful air. I began to be harsh with her as at Balbec, at the time of my first fit of jealousy. Her face reflected her disappointment, and in reproaching her I used the same arguments that had been so often advanced against me by my parents when I was small, and that had appeared so unintelligent and cruel to my misunderstood childhood. 'No, in spite of your gloomy look,' I said to Albertine, 'I can't feel sorry for you; I should feel sorry for you if you were ill, if you were in trouble, if you had suffered some bereavement; not that you would mind in the least, I dare say, considering your expenditure of false sensibility over nothing. Besides, I'm not very impressed by the sensibility of people who pretend to be so fond of us and are quite incapable of doing us the smallest favour, and whose minds wander so that they forget to deliver the letter we have entrusted to them on which our whole future depends.'

A great part of what we say being no more than a recitation from memory, I had often heard these words uttered by my mother, who (always ready to explain to me that one ought not to confuse genuine sensibility with sentimentality, what the Germans, whose language she greatly admired despite my grandfather's loathing for that nation, called *Empfindung* and *Empfindelei*) once, when I was in tears, had gone so far as to tell me that Nero was probably highly-strung and was none the better for that. Indeed, like those plants which bifurcate as they grow, side by side with the sensitive boy which was all that I had been, there was now a man of the opposite sort, full of common sense, of severity towards the morbid sensibility of others, a man resembling what my parents had been to me. No doubt, as each of us is obliged to continue in himself the life of his forebears, the level-headed, caustic individual who did not exist in me at the start had joined forces with the sensitive one, and it was natural that I should become in my turn what my parents had been to me. What is more, at the moment when this new personality took shape in me, he found his language ready made in the memory of the sarcastic, scolding things that had been said to me, that I must now say to others, and that came so naturally to my lips, either because I evoked them through mimicry and association of memories, or because the delicate and mysterious incrustations of genetic energy had traced in me unawares, as upon the leaf of a plant, the same intonations, the same gestures, the same attitudes as had been characteristic of those from whom I sprang. Sometimes, playing the sage when talking to Albertine, I seemed to be hearing my grandmother. Indeed it often happened to my mother (so many obscure unconscious currents caused everything in me even down to the tiniest movements of my fingers to be drawn into the same cycles as my parents) to imagine that it was my father at the door, so similar was my knock to his.

Moreover the coupling of contrary elements is the law of life, the principle of fertilisation, and, as we shall see, the cause of many misfortunes. As a rule we detest what resembles ourselves, and our own faults when observed in another person exasperate us. How much the more does a man who has passed the age at which one instinctively displays them, a man who, for instance, has maintained an expression of icy calm through the most aggravating moments, execrate those same faults if it is another man, younger or simpler or stupider, who displays them! There are sensitive people for whom merely to see in other people's eyes the tears which they themselves have held back is infuriating. It is excessive similarity that, in spite of affection, and sometimes all the more the greater the affection, causes division to reign in families.

Possibly in myself, as in many other people, the second man that I had become was simply another aspect of the first, excitable and sensitive where he himself was concerned, a sage mentor to others. Perhaps it was so also with my parents according to whether they were considered in relation to me or in themselves. In the case of my grandmother and mother it was only too clear that their severity towards me was deliberate on their part and indeed cost them dear, but perhaps even my father's coldness too was only an external aspect of his sensibility. For it was perhaps the human truth of this twofold aspect—the one concerned with the inner life, the other with social relations—that was expressed in a remark which seemed to me at the time as false in substance as it was commonplace in form, when someone said of my father: 'Beneath his icy exterior, he conceals an extraordinary sensibility; the truth is that he's ashamed of his feelings.' Did it not in fact conceal incessant secret storms, that calm of his, interspersed at times with sententious reflections and ironical comments on the awkward manifestations of sensibility, which now I too affected in my relations with everyone and above all never swerved from, in certain circumstances, with Albertine?

I really believe that I came near that day to making up my mind to break with her and to set out for Venice. What bound me anew in my chains had to do with Normandy, not that she showed any inclination to go to that region where I had been jealous of her (for it was my good fortune that her plans never impinged upon the painful zones in my memory), but because when I happened to say to her: 'It's as though I were speaking to you about your aunt's friend who lived at Infreville,' she replied angrily, delighted—like everyone in an argument who is anxious to muster as many points as possible on his side—to show me that I was in the wrong and herself in the right: 'But my aunt never knew anybody at Infreville, and I've never been near the place.' She had forgotten the lie that she had told me one afternoon about the touchy lady with whom she simply must go and have tea, even if by visiting this lady she were to forfeit my friendship and shorten her own life. I did not remind her of her lie. But it shattered me. And once again I postponed our rupture to another day. A person has no need of sincerity, nor even of skill in lying, in order to be loved. Here I mean by love reciprocal torture.

I saw nothing reprehensible that evening in speaking to her as my grandmother—that mirror of perfection—used to speak to me, nor, when I told her that I would escort her to the Verdurins', in having adopted the brusque manner of my father, who would never inform us of any decision except in a manner calculated to cause us the maximum of agitation, out of all proportion to the decision itself. So that it was easy for him to call us absurd for appearing so distressed by so small a matter, our distress corresponding in reality to the perturbation that he had aroused in us. And if—like the inflexible wisdom of my grandmother—these arbitrary whims of my father's had been passed on to me to complement the sensitive nature to which they had so long remained alien and, throughout my whole childhood, had caused so much suffering, that sensitive nature informed them very exactly as to the points at which they could most effectively be aimed: there is no better informer than a reformed thief, or a subject of the nation one is fighting. In certain untruthful families, a brother who has come to call without any apparent reason and makes some casual inquiry on the doorstep as he leaves, appearing scarcely to listen to the answer, indicates thereby to his brother that this inquiry was the sole object of his visit, for the brother is quite familiar with that air of detachment, those words uttered as though in parentheses and at the last moment, having frequently had recourse to them himself. Similarly, there are pathological families, kindred sensibilities, fraternal temperaments, initiated into that mute language which enables the members of a family to understand each other without speaking. Thus who can be more nerve-racking than a neurotic? And then there may have been a deeper and more general cause for my behaviour in these cases. In those brief but inevitable moments when we hate someone we love—moments which last sometimes for a whole lifetime in the case of people we do not love—we do not wish to appear kind in order not to be pitied, but at once as unpleasant and as happy as possible so that our happiness may be truly hateful and wound to the very soul the occasional or permanent enemy. To how many people have I not untruthfully maligned myself, simply in order that my 'successes' might seem to them the more immoral and infuriate them the more! The proper thing to do would be to take the opposite course, to show without arrogance that we have generous feelings, instead of taking such pains to hide them. And this would be easy if we were capable of never hating, of always loving. For then we should be so happy to say only the things that can make other people happy, melt their hearts, make them love us.

True, I felt some remorse at being so insufferable to Albertine, and said to myself: 'If I didn't love her, she would be more grateful to me, for I wouldn't be nasty to her; but no, it would be the same in the end, for I should also be less nice.' And I might, in order to justify myself, have told her that I loved her. But the avowal of that love, apart from the fact that it would have told Albertine nothing new, would perhaps have made her colder towards me than the harshness and deceit for which love was the sole excuse. To be harsh and deceitful to the person whom we love is so natural! If the interest that we show towards other people does not prevent us from being gentle towards them and complying with their wishes, it is because our interest is not sincere. Other people leave us indifferent, and indifference does not prompt us to unkindness.

The evening was drawing to a close. Before Albertine went to bed, there was no time to lose if we wished to make peace, to renew our embraces. Neither of us had yet taken the initiative.

Meanwhile, feeling that in any case she was angry with me, I took the opportunity of mentioning Esther Lévy. 'Bloch tells me,' I said untruthfully, 'that you're a great friend of his cousin Esther.'

'I shouldn't know her if I saw her,' said Albertine with a vague look.

'I've seen her photograph,' I continued angrily. I did not look at Albertine as I said this, so that I did not see her expression, which would have been her sole reply, for she said nothing.

It was no longer the peace of my mother's kiss at Combray that I felt when I was with Albertine on these evenings, but, on the contrary, the anguish of those on which my mother scarcely bade me good-night, or even did not come up to my room at all, either because she was cross with me or was kept downstairs by guests. This anguish— not merely its transposition into love but this anguish itself—which for a time had specialised in love and which, when the separation, the division of the passions occurred, had been assigned to love alone, now seemed once more to be extending to them all, to have become indivisible again as in my childhood, as though all my feelings, which trembled at the thought of my not being able to keep Albertine by my bedside, at once as a mistress, a sister, a daughter, and as a mother too, of whose regular good-night kiss I was beginning once more to feel the childish need, had begun to coalesce, to become unified in the premature evening of my life which seemed fated to be as short as a winter day. But if I felt the same anguish as in my childhood, the different person who caused me to feel it, the difference in the feeling she inspired in me, the very transformation in my character, made it impossible for me to demand its appeasement from Albertine as in the old days from my mother. I could no longer say: 'I'm unhappy.' I confined myself, with a heavy heart, to speaking of inconsequential matters that took me no further towards a happy solution. I waded knee-deep in painful platitudes. And with that intellectual egoism which, if some insignificant fact happens to have a bearing on our love, makes us pay great respect to the person who has discovered it, as fortuitously perhaps as the fortune-teller who has foretold some trivial event which has afterwards come to pass, I came near to regarding Françoise as more inspired than Bergotte and Elstir because she had said to me at Balbec: 'That girl will bring you nothing but trouble.'

Every minute brought me nearer to Albertine's good-night, which at length she said. But that evening her kiss, from which she herself was absent and which made no impression on me, left me so anxious that, with a throbbing heart, I watched her make her way to the door, thinking: 'If I'm to find a pretext for calling her back, keeping her here, making peace with her, I must be quick; only a few steps and she will be out of the room, only two, now one, she's turning the handle; she's opening the door, it's too late, she has shut it behind her!' But perhaps it was not too late after all. As in the old days at Combray when my mother had left me without soothing me with her kiss, I wanted to rush after Albertine, I felt that there would be no peace for me until I had seen her again, that this renewed encounter would turn into something tremendous which it had not been before and that—if I did not succeed by my own efforts in ridding myself of this misery—I might perhaps acquire the shameful habit of going to beg from Albertine. I sprang out of bed when she was already in her room, I paced up and down the corridor, hoping that she would come out of her room and call me; I stood stock-still outside her door for fear of failing to hear some faint summons, I returned for a moment to my own room to see whether she might not by some lucky chance have forgotten her handkerchief, her bag, something which I might have appeared to be afraid of her needing during the night, and which would have given me an excuse for going to her room. No, there was nothing. I returned to my station outside her door, but the crack beneath it no longer showed any light. Albertine had put out the light, she was in bed; I remained there motionless, hoping for some lucky accident which did not occur; and long afterwards, frozen, I returned to bestow myself between my own sheets and cried for the rest of the night.

But on certain such evenings I had recourse to a ruse which won me Albertine's kiss. Knowing how quickly sleep came to her as soon as she lay down (she knew it also, for, instinctively, before lying down, she would take off the slippers which I had given her, and her ring which she placed by the bedside, as she did in her own room when she went to bed), knowing how heavy her sleep was, how affectionate her awakening, I would find an excuse for going to look for something and make her lie down on my bed. When I returned she would be asleep and I saw before me the other woman that she became whenever one saw her full-face. But her personality quickly changed when I lay down beside her and saw her again in profile. I could take her head, lift it up, press her face to my lips, put her arms round my neck, and she would continue to sleep, like a watch that never stops, like an animal that stays in whatever position you put it in, like a climbing plant, a convolvulus which continues to thrust out its tendrils whatever support you give it. Only her breathing was altered by each touch of my fingers, as though she were an instrument on which I was playing and from which I extracted modulations by drawing different notes from one after another of its strings. My jealousy subsided, for I felt that Albertine had become a creature that breathes and is nothing else besides, as was indicated by the regular suspiration in which is expressed that pure physiological function which, wholly fluid, has the solidity neither of speech nor of silence; and, in its ignorance of all evil, drawn seemingly rather from a hollowed reed than from a human being, that breath, truly paradisiacal to me who at such moments felt Albertine to be withdrawn from everything, not only physically but morally, was the pure song of the angels. And yet, in that breathing, I thought to myself of a sudden that perhaps many names of people, borne on the stream of memory, must be revolving.

Sometimes indeed the human voice was added to that music. Albertine would murmur a few words. How I longed to catch their meaning! It would happen that the name of a person of whom we had been speaking and who had aroused my jealousy would come to her lips, but without making me unhappy, for the memory that it brought with it seemed to be only that of the conversations that she had had with me on the subject. One evening, however, when with her eyes still shut she half awoke, she said tenderly, addressing me: 'Andrée.' I concealed my emotion. 'You're dreaming, I'm not Andrée,' I said to her, smiling. She smiled also: 'Of course not, I wanted to ask you what Andrée said to you this evening.' 'I assumed that you used to lie beside her like that.' 'Oh no, never,' she said. But, before making this reply, she had hidden her face for a moment in her hands. So her silences were merely screens, her surface affection merely kept beneath the surface a thousand memories which would have rent my heart, her life was full of those incidents the good-natured, bantering account of which forms one's daily gossip at the expense of other people, people who do not matter, but which, so long as a woman remains buried in the depths of one's heart, seem to us so precious a revelation of her life that, for the privilege of exploring that underlying world, we would gladly sacrifice our own. Then her sleep would seem to me a marvellous and magic world in which at certain moments there rises from the depths of the barely translucent element the avowal of a secret which we shall not understand. But as a rule, when Albertine was asleep, she seemed to have recaptured her innocence. In the attitude which I had imposed upon her, but which in her sleep she had speedily made her own, she seemed to trust herself to me. Her face had lost any expression of cunning or vulgarity, and between herself and me, towards whom she raised her arm, on whom she rested her hand, there seemed to be an absolute surrender, an indissoluble attachment. Her sleep moreover did not separate her from me and allowed her to retain the consciousness of our affection; its effect was rather to abolish everything else; I would kiss her, tell her that I was going to take a turn outside, and she would half-open her eyes and say to me with a look of surprise— for the hour was indeed late—'But where are you off to, my darling——'(calling me by my Christian name), and at once fall asleep again. Her sleep was no more than a sort of blotting out of the rest of her life, an even silence over which from time to time familiar words of tenderness would pass in their flight. By putting these words together, one might have arrived at the unalloyed conversation, the secret intimacy of a pure love. This calm slumber delighted me, as a mother, reckoning it a virtue, is delighted by her child's sound sleep. And her sleep was indeed that of a child. Her awakening also, so natural and so loving, before she even knew where she was, that I sometimes asked myself with dread whether she had been in the habit, before coming to live with me, of not sleeping alone but of finding, when she opened her eyes, someone lying by her side. But her childlike grace was more striking. Like a mother again, I marvelled that she should always awake in such a good humour. After a few moments she would recover consciousness, would utter charming words, unconnected with one another, mere twitterings. By a sort of reversal of roles, her throat, which as a rule one seldom remarked, now almost startlingly beautiful, had acquired the immense importance which her eyes, by being closed in sleep, had lost, her eyes, my regular interlocutors to which I could no longer address myself after the lids had closed over them. Just as the closed lids impart an innocent, grave beauty to the face by suppressing all that the eyes express only too plainly, there was in the words, not devoid of meaning but interrupted by moments of silence, which Albertine uttered as she awoke, a pure beauty of a kind that is not constantly tarnished, as is conversation, by habits of speech, stale repetitions, traces of familiar defects. Moreover, when I had decided to wake Albertine, I would have been able to do so without fear, knowing that her awakening would bear no relation to the evening that we had passed together, but would emerge from her sleep as morning emerges from night. As soon as she had begun to open her eyes with a smile, she would have offered me her lips, and before she had even said a word, I would have savoured their freshness, as soothing as that of a garden still silent before the break of day.

MARCEL PROUST was a French novelist and critic who is frequently named as the most important writer of the twentieth century. A socialite amongst France's fading aristocracy, he published essays on art and literary criticism before embarking on one of modern literature's most ambitious and influential projects, his multi-volume novel, *In Search of Lost Time*.

Although Proust's work is best known for madeleines and its exploration of memory, jealousy is an ever-present force through-out. Volume V of *In Search of Lost Time* (from which this book is taken) has at its heart the ill-fated love affair between the novel's narrator and his childhood sweetheart, Albertine. The depiction of jealousy that eventually consumes them is said to be closely modelled on Proust's own failed romances.

Plagued by ill health, Proust retreated from Parisian society for the last years of his life. He died in 1922.

RECOMMENDED BOOKS BY MARCEL PROUST:

*In Search of Lost Time, Volumes I–VI*

# Is there more to love than Jealousy?

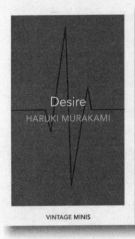

Desire
HARUKI MURAKAMI

VINTAGE MINIS

Eating
NIGELLA LAWSON

VINTAGE MINIS

Home
SALMAN RUSHDIE

VINTAGE MINIS

Babies
ANNE ENRIGHT

VINTAGE MINIS

## VINTAGE MINIS

The Vintage Minis bring you the world's greatest writers on the experiences that make us human. These stylish, entertaining little books explore the whole spectrum of life – from birth to death, and everything in between. Which means there's something here for everyone, whatever your story.